ALWAYS REMEMBER

Cece Meng *illustrated by* Jago

PHILOMEL BOOKS

IN THE END, on his very last day, Old Turtle swam his last swim and took his last breath. With his life complete, the gentle waves took him away.

By dawn, everyone who knew Old Turtle knew he was gone.

The turtles playing in
the reef remembered how
he taught them to swim.

Old Turtle had been a good teacher.

And the turtles would
always remember.

The broad-backed humpback whale
remembered how Old Turtle swam
alongside of her and kept her company
when she became separated from her pod.
Old Turtle had been a good friend.

And the whale would always remember.

The sea otters remembered how Old Turtle would dive and play with them and make them laugh. Old Turtle had loved to have fun.

And the otters would always remember.

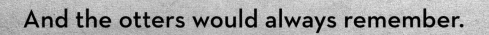

The dolphins remembered how
Old Turtle was curious about the
unknown and bravely swam far
out to sea.

Old Turtle explored the darkest of the waters and discovered glittery jewels to show his friends.

And the dolphins would
always remember.

Once, a terrible storm
tossed and turned the
ocean for three long days
and nights. A starfish was
torn from her rock and
swept away.

When the waves became calm
again, Old Turtle looked for her and
found her and carried her home.

And the starfish would
always remember.

When Old Turtle found a manatee tangled in a fishing net, he snipped and pulled and would not stop until the manatee was free.

The manatee told the story to his children, and they told the story to their children.

Old Turtle would never be forgotten.

Once upon a time,
there was an Old Turtle.

He was a wonderful teacher and friend.

He loved to laugh and have fun.

He explored the unknown and discovered great things.

He showed kindness and strength.

And he made his world a better place.

When Old Turtle died, the ocean took him back.

But what he left behind was only the beginning.

To my parents
—Cece Meng

For Alex, Lily and Rudy
—Jago

PHILOMEL BOOKS
an imprint of Penguin Random House LLC
375 Hudson Street, New York, NY 10014

Text copyright © 2016 by Cece Meng. Illustrations copyright © 2016 by Jago Silver.
Penguin supports copyright. Copyright fuels creativity, encourages diverse voices, promotes free speech, and creates
a vibrant culture. Thank you for buying an authorized edition of this book and for complying with copyright laws by not
reproducing, scanning, or distributing any part of it in any form without permission. You are supporting writers and allowing
Penguin to continue to publish books for every reader.
Philomel Books is a registered trademark of Penguin Random House LLC.

Library of Congress Cataloging-in-Publication Data
Meng, Cece.
Always remember / Cece Meng. pages cm Summary: When Old Turtle dies and is taken back by the sea, his friends
remember that he was a wonderful teacher and friend who made his world a better place. [1. Death—Fiction. 2. Conduct of
life—Fiction. 3. Sea turtles—Fiction. 4. Turtles—Fiction. 5. Marine animals—Fiction.] I. Title. PZ7.M5268Alw 2016 [E]—dc23
2015001902

Manufactured in China by RR Donnelley Asia Printing Solutions Ltd.   ISBN 978-0-399-16809-3   10 9 8

Edited by Jill Santopolo.   Design by Siobhán Gallagher.   Text set in 20-point Neutraface 2 Text.   Art was done digitally.